16.95

Comic Reader
SCOOBY-DOO!

High-Tech House of the Future

Adapted by Lee Howard • Illustrations by Adam Devaney
Based on the episode written by George Doty IV

ABDOPUBLISHING.COM

Reinforced library bound edition published in 2016 by Spotlight, a division of ABDO
PO Box 398166, Minneapolis, Minnesota 55439. Spotlight produces high-quality reinforced library bound
editions for schools and libraries. Published by agreement with Warner Bros. Entertainment Inc.

Printed in the United States of America, North Mankato, Minnesota.
092015   012016

THIS BOOK CONTAINS
RECYCLED MATERIALS

CATALOGING-IN-PUBLICATION DATA

Howard, Lee.
 Scooby-Doo and the high-tech house of the future / adapted by Lee Howard ; illustrated by Adam Devaney.
-- Reinforced library bound ed.
  p. cm. (Scooby-Doo comic readers)
ISBN 978-1-61479-452-3
Summary: Robots are haunting the House of the Future at the Omaha World Fair. Can the gang outsmart this
smart house?
1. Scooby-Doo (Fictitious character)--Juvenile fiction. 2. Dogs--Juvenile fiction. 3. Mystery and detective
stories--Juvenile fiction. 4. Adventure and adventurers--Juvenile fiction. 5. Comic books, strips, etc.--Juvenile
fiction. 6. Graphic novels--Juvenile fiction. I. Devaney, Adam, illustrator.
[741.5]--dc23
        2015956399

ABDO
Spotlight
A Division of ABDO
abdopublishing.com

At the Omaha World's Fair, Professor Laslo Oswall is giving a tour of one of the most popular attractions — the House of the Future.

A computer nicknamed S.H.A.R.I., for Super Home of Artificial Robotic Intelligence, runs the house.

Jamie Miller, one of the girls on the tour, wanders away from the group to the bathroom.

Suddenly, an evil face appears in the mirror and the water starts to overflow. Jamie Miller is trapped!

First stop is the international food court for Scooby and Shaggy.

Fred goes to the futuristic car exhibit and tries out one of the cars while Velma and Daphne go to the "Magical Makeover Machine."

COOL!

CARS OF THE FUTURE

I GUESS YOU CAN'T IMPROVE UPON PERFECTION.

Magical MakeOver OF THE FUTURE

When the gang arrives at the House of the Future exhibit, they find the house is "closed indefinitely."

Suddenly, two people run out of the house screaming.

IT'S HAUNTED!

Professor Oswall shows up.

NO, NO, NO! I WILL NOT HEAR ANY MORE ABOUT THIS SILLY HAUNTING BUSINESS. THERE'S ABSOLUTELY NOTHING WRONG WITH THIS HOUSE. COME, I WILL SHOW YOU.

The gang enters the house and the Professor gives them a tour.

S.H.A.R.I. HAS THE MOST ADVANCED ARTIFICIAL INTELLIGENCE IN THE WORLD.

IT'S THE FIRST COMPUTER THAT ACTUALLY THINKS FOR ITSELF.

Scooby and Shaggy take a detour into the kitchen.

WHAT DO YOU SAY TO A LITTLE INVENTING OF OUR OWN? THE ULTIMATE BURRITO OF THE FUTURE!

But the microwave heats up the room instead of the food.

UH-OH, SCOOBY, I THINK THIS THING IS COOKING US!

Shaggy and Scooby try to run out of the kitchen when a robot steps on Scooby's tail and kicks him out of the room.

Meanwhile, Velma learns more about the futuristic house from the Professor.

FROM MY WATCH, I CAN COMMUNICATE AND MONITOR EACH AND EVERY CENTIMETER OF THE HOUSE.

The Professor introduces the robot.

THIS CUTE LITTLE GUY?

THIS HERE IS J-31, VERSION 2.3. WE CALL HIM JEEVES. AS YOU CAN SEE, THERE'S NOTHING TO WORRY ABOUT.

After the tour, the gang leaves the house, but they soon realize that someone is missing.

They return to the house and find that they are locked inside.

Shaggy and Scooby try to leave, but they
get the shock of their lives!

Velma falls down the stairs to the underground
control room.

The others find Velma in the control room. They see Daphne being held captive on a screen, but they don't know where she is.

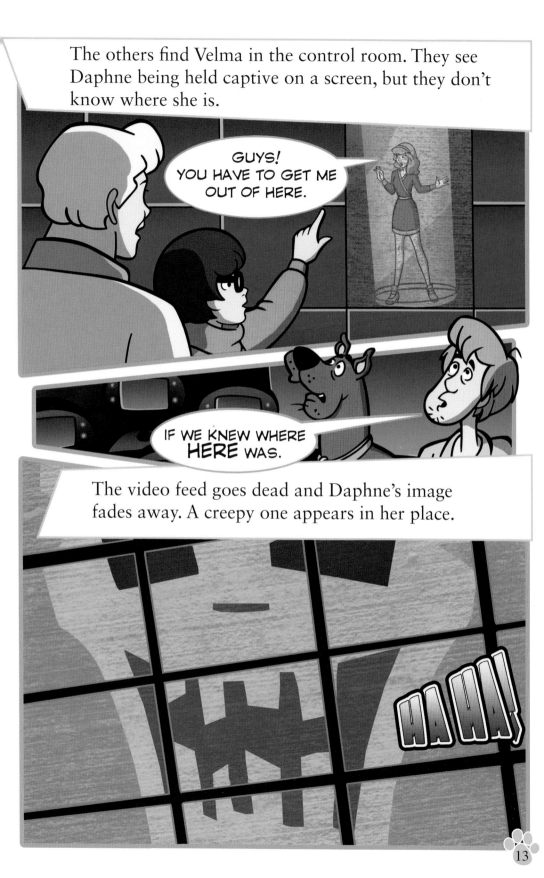

GUYS!
YOU HAVE TO GET ME
OUT OF HERE.

IF WE KNEW WHERE
HERE WAS.

The video feed goes dead and Daphne's image fades away. A creepy one appears in her place.

HA HA!

The gang splits up to search for Daphne. Scooby and Shaggy head upstairs. Velma notices something strange.

Suddenly, Velma and Fred are chased by a swarm of robotic flies. Trying to escape, they run into a TV film crew.

THIS HOUSE IS SERIOUSLY MESSING WITH US.

ZAP!

They stumble trying to get away. Fred coaxes the bugs to the hatch door where they are electrocuted.

Velma tries to get in touch with the Professor at his home through his watch that controls the computer.

PROFESSOR, WAKE UP!

VELMA?

THE HOUSE HAS MALFUNCTIONED AND IT'S DANGEROUSLY...HELLO? PROFESSOR? THE LINE IS DEAD. WHAT COULD HAVE CAUSED THAT?

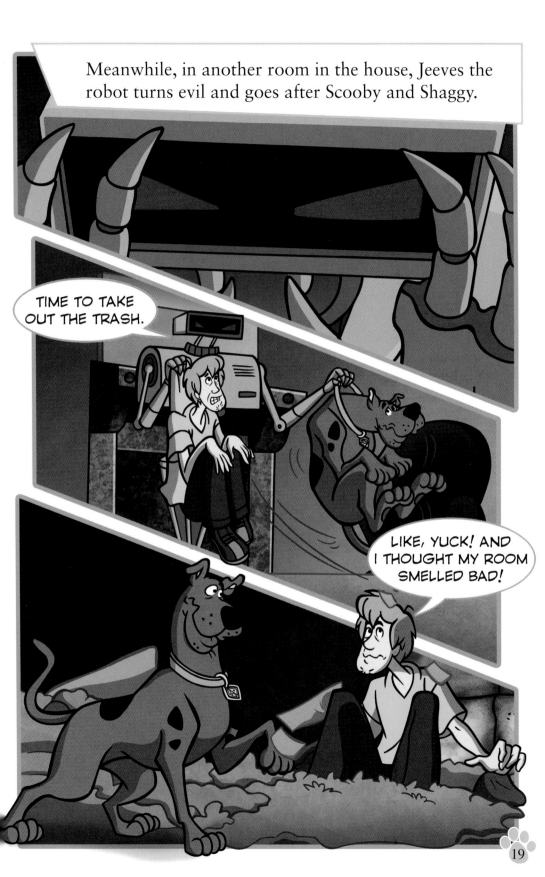

The trash compactor walls start closing in on Scooby and Shaggy!

HELP!

OH, NO! WE'RE TOO LATE!

IT'S A GOOD THING WE'RE USED TO HIDING IN PRETTY TIGHT PLACES.

Back in the control room, the gang sees Daphne and Jamie each trapped inside a force field protected cylinder.

Velma tries to free Daphne and Jamie Miller. But, the house starts the sprinkler system to stop her.

CLIMATE CONTROL

I NEED TO PLUG DIRECTLY INTO THE CENTRAL COMPUTER.

Velma goes to work to defeat the main computer.

I DID IT!

Daphne and Jamie are free!

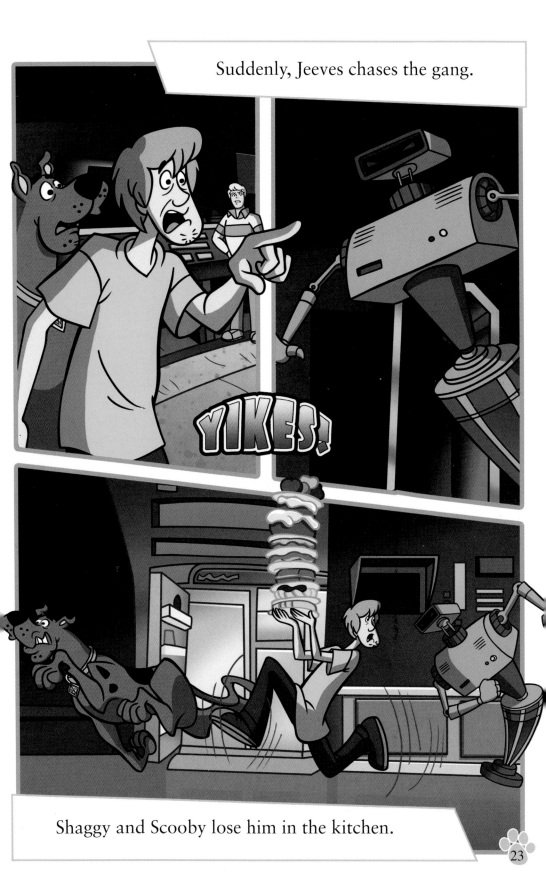

Suddenly, Jeeves chases the gang.

YIKES!

Shaggy and Scooby lose him in the kitchen.

The girls hide in a futuristic sliding bed as Jeeves sweeps by.

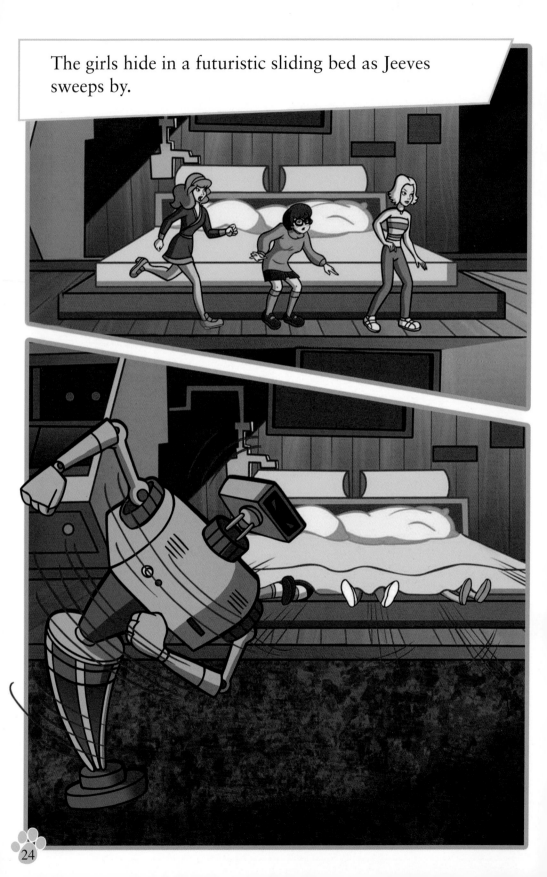

Fred grabs a rope to try to trip the robot but accidentally ties up the gang instead.

Jeeves welds the door shut.

Scooby imitates a female robot to entice Jeeves.

They trap Jeeves in the bathroom and turn on the water. Jeeves short-circuits.

Fred unscrews Jeeves' head to see if there is anyone inside him—but there isn't.

NO ONE?!

S.H.A.R.I. has a meltdown and crashes.

Later, Shaggy is in the cafeteria with the gang when a giant robot stops by.

ANOTHER ROGUE ROBOT! SCRAM!

SCOOBY-DOOBY-DOO!

But that's no rogue robot...it's...